A Guide for How to Be LGBTQ+ Parents

Teach Children About Tolerance, Love, and Acceptance in a Polarized World

Frank Dixon

from various sources. Please consult a licensed professional before attempting any techniques outlined in this book.

By reading this document, the reader agrees that under no circumstances is the author responsible for any losses, direct or indirect, that are incurred as a result of the use of the information contained within this document, including, but not limited to, errors, omissions, or inaccuracies.

Before we begin, I have something special waiting for you. An action-packed 1 page printout with a few quick & easy tips taken from this book that you can start using today to become a better parent right now!

It's my gift to you, free of cost. Think of it as my way of saying thank you to you for purchasing this book.

Claim your download of Profoundly Positive Parenting with Frank Dixon by scanning the QR code below and join my mailing list.

Sign up below to grab your free copy, print it out and hang it on the fridge!

Sign Up By Scanning The QR Code With Your Phone's Camera To Be Redirected To A Page To Enter Your Email And Receive INSTANT Access To Your Download

Before we jump in, I'd like to express my gratitude. I know this mustn't be the first book you came across and yet you still decided to give it a read. There are numerous courses and guides you could have picked instead that promise to make you an ideal and well-rounded parent while raising your children to be the best they can be.

But for some reason, mine stood out from the rest and this makes me the happiest person on the planet right now. If you stick with it, I promise this will be a worthwhile read.

In the pages that follow, you're going to learn the best parenting skills so that your child can grow to become the best version of themselves and in doing so experience a meaningful understanding of what it means to be an effective parent.

Notable Quotes About Parenting

"Children Must Be Taught How To Think, Not What To Think."

– Margaret Mead

"It's easier to build strong children than to fix broken men [or women]."

- Frederick Douglass

"Truly great friends are hard to find, difficult to leave, and impossible to forget."

– George Randolf

"Nothing in life is to be feared, it is only to be understood. Now is the time to understand more, so that we may fear less."

– Scientist Marie Curie

Table of Contents

Introduction

People have had issues with something different and new. It is no wonder gender stereotyping is so common. It speaks of beliefs that males and females should have some distinct characteristics. Men are seen as macho, strong-willed, and breadwinners whereas women are viewed as feminine, gentle, and emotional. Although these characteristics vary, it wouldn't be wrong to say that we have stigmatized sexual orientations and gender identities. We have assigned different roles to males and females and expect them to fulfill those roles—no matter what.

However, times are changing, and so should we.

Today, a three-year-old toddler may show evidence of some rudimentary knowledge about the activities and objects associated with each sex. They know action figures and cars are for boys to play with, and dolls and stuffed animals for girls. They know that men can be firefighters, astronauts, and police officers whereas women are homemakers, chefs, and teachers. This knowledge about the activities and occupations of gender stereotypes develops quickly during the preschool years and kindergarten.

But, when it comes to adolescence, children begin to question who they are and how they can define themselves. Part of the answer they seek so eagerly lies within their sexual self. They question their sexual orientation and gender identity often.

You might be wondering why we keep using sexual orientation and gender identity as two different words. Aren't they the same?

No, absolutely not!

An individual's sexual orientation refers to whom they are attracted to romantically and sexually. Children can be any of the following:

- Heterosexual: where they are attracted to only the other binary gender
- Gay: attracted to only one of the two genders
- Bisexual: attracted to both binary genders
- Pansexual: attracted to those of any gender
- Asexual: attracted to no gender, etc.

Preteens and teen years are when children become aware of their sexual orientation and preference. They find out they have a crush on someone of the same gender or have no feelings whatsoever toward anyone at all.

Gender identity, on the other hand, is one's inner sense of being male, female, or both. For transgender people, the identity they are given at birth doesn't match their sex. They feel like a stranger in their own body. Children become aware of their gender identity sooner. Children as young as three can know for sure who they are: a boy or a girl. Many transgender children recall feelings strange and unfamiliar with the sex they were assigned. Others didn't experience the feeling until later in life.

For parents, navigating the new normal and making peace with the person their children wish to be is a difficult one. Conservative thinking, accompanied by years of a brainwashed perspective toward the LGBTQ+ community, scares them. They don't want a child resonating with the same community within their homes. However, family support and acceptance are pivotal for the mental and emotional well-being of the child. According to a 2012 survey, 92% of LGBT teens don't feel welcomed or accepted for being gay, lesbian, bisexual, or transgender (Griffin, 2012). They are verbally harassed and called names. They are told to rethink and readjust with the rest of the world when they were born to stand out. They often feel like an alien among their friends, family, and community. Parents expect them to deny or hide the fact that they are different; this is sad, to say the least.

But what else can you expect from someone with little to no knowledge about how to accept a child that identifies as diverse, let alone raise one? There is a fear of rejection by community members. They are worried about their child's mental and emotional safety. They are worried that they will be bullied, and their parenting methods will be questioned.

If you happen to be one of those parents that has just received the news about your child's different sexual orientation/gender identity and are worried that you don't know what to do next, read along. First, allow yourself to process this new piece of information. Don't let your initial reactions be of worry, concern, or worse, rejection.

Next, continue to read on, as this book offers promising advice to become a proud parent of an LGBTQ+ child.

Chapter 1:

It All Starts With Education

For a child, coming out to their parents, friends, and extended family is ending a lifelong journey of being someone else and gearing up the courage to be who they are. It involves acknowledgment of one's true identity, whether through gender modification or sexual preference. For some, it can take years to muster up the courage whereas some never reveal.

For any child, wanting to come out depends on a number of factors—the first being their parent's reaction. They are fearful of how their parents will take in the information. They are worried if their love and affection would change toward them. They think they won't see them the way they did anymore.

All this thinking happens when they sense a discouraging narrative in the house toward the LGBTQ+ community. Perhaps they saw you speaking negatively about the LGBTQ+ community with a friend on the phone or while watching the news. Perhaps they sensed a difference in treatment toward your neighbors because they identify as different, or maybe you just had no opinion whatsoever about the LGBTQ+ people.

But remember: Every parent should aspire to help their children achieve their dreams and passions. They want to see them succeed in their lives, be happy, and have meaningful relationships. They want to give them the best of the world and never stop loving them.

So why does this perception change the second a child decides to tell you who they really want to be? Why do some parents go into a state of shock and then, due to sadness and feelings of shame, cover their faces? Why can't they make peace with the reality that their child has been living in?

The journey to acknowledgment, acceptance, and admiration begins with knowing your child and who they are. Then comes educating yourself and others about why the way you see your child shouldn't change—regardless of their gender identity/sexual orientation.

Know Thy Child

Taking the time to understand and acknowledge your child is something that every parent should learn. Parental care and attention play a key role in guiding and nurturing positive habits in children and helping them mature. No two children can have the same personality. Some are naturally shy while others are the life of the party. Some are observant of the smallest changes while others don't notice even the biggest of changes in the first attempt. Some are outspoken and straightforward while others think things through a lot. Some are intuitive while others go with the flow. Some take risks while others never step out of their comfort zone. Unique personality traits remain the same forever—even when the circumstances change. We can change a habit, but we can't change nature.

One of the best ways to observe and learn about your child is through observation—not just when they are with you but also when they are alone or with others. How do they form bonds? What objects and things interest them? What does their browser history look like? What hobbies and passions do they follow? What games and activities make them happy? Look at how they interact with their friends, educators, family, friends, and you. Do you notice any consistent traits? Do they find adjusting to change simple or time-consuming? What opinions do they hold of others around them? How accepting or non-accepting are they of people from diverse backgrounds, communities, and cultures?

Such questions allow you to know them better.

Speaking of their sexual or gender preference, it isn't something that a child just makes up stories about. It isn't something they can change or get over. People don't choose their sexual orientation. Trying to change who you are is the same as trying to change your eye color or height. There is nothing you can do about either, but you must make peace with it.

Statistically speaking, 10% of people are gay (Spiegelhalter, 2015). "Gay" is a common term people use to refer to people who identify as LGBTQ+. It isn't a disability or mental disorder, which is why you must ditch any such notions and misconceptions firstly. No amount of evidence has been able to convince that being gay is linked with early childhood experiences, the upbringing of a child, or parenting style. Efforts by religious groups and conversion therapies, which propose that gays can be turned into straight people, have proven ineffective and harmful.

Signs That Predicts Sexual Orientation in Toddlers

We have all been aware of the stereotypes—an unusually dressed teenager with dyed hair, smudged eyeliner under the eyes, and a delicate yet effeminate air about themselves. There's also a keen interest in dolls and women's dresses and shoes, accompanied by a strong distaste for rough play with the boys their age. Something similar holds for the girls where they dress outwardly boyish, love to play with tools, don't want to be told down, and are always ready for a tussle with the boys. Give them dolls, dresses, and makeup to play with, and they will vomit at the sight of them. No feminine features or elegance can be associated with them.

Many parents fear these behaviors in children. They know that these are loathed and often spoken of as harbingers of homosexuality. However, playing dress-up or wanting to do "boy things" isn't a reliable sign of adult homosexuality. The most reliable signs of adult homosexuality in children are sets of behavioral indicators gay people have in common.

These include the difference in the domain of play. Boys have a natural tendency to engage in developmental rough and tumble play. Girls, on the other hand, prefer the company of dolls and tea parties with them. The type of toys children prefer to play with also indicates sex difference where boys naturally gravitate toward action figures and machine guns, and girls are more drawn to hyperfeminized figurines and makeup. Both males and females enjoy pretend play; however, the roles within the imagination context are gender-segregated. Girls enact roles of their mothers, teachers, ballerinas, and princesses whereas boys like to pretend to be soldiers, police officers, and superheroes. This is one reason why boys prefer to play with boys, and girls prefer to play with girls.

However, this isn't confined to playing dress-up or holding a hockey stick in hand. We must keep in mind that not every child which acts against their stereotyped role has an identity crisis. Some are simply curious and imaginative. Research proves this, too: In a 2008 study, lead researcher, Kelly Drummond, interviewed 25 adult females referred for an assessment by their parents at a mental health clinic when they were between the ages of three and twelve. They all suffered from several diagnostic indicators of gender identity disorder. They all showed the usual "symptoms" like wanting a male playmate, dressing up in shorts and pants, favoring rough play, etc. They believed they were assigned the wrong gender at birth. Some of them were so sure that they refused to pee sitting down and knew they would eventually grow a phallus at some point in time. Yet only 12% of them grew up to have gender dysphoria.

The point is that there is no sure way of knowing your child's gender identity and sexual orientation. Some telltale signs may indicate their preference, but it can only be an exploratory phase they are going through. The only sure way to tell if your child is gay, lesbian, bi, or transsexual is by asking them. If they appear confused, provide them with age-appropriate exposure through media and books.

Education for You and Others

Knowing your sexual orientation and identity is something that children and teenagers recognize, with some doubt, at a young age. Some had same-sex crushes and couldn't explain the reason behind that attraction. By the time they reached middle school, this infatuation became stronger and made them admit their sexual orientation.

However, not many children reveal it to others. They assume it is a phase of experimentation where hormones are to blame, but they begin to question their orientation and realize they had felt this awkwardness for quite a while.

This journey of becoming aware and accepting one's true identity takes time. At first, it feels wrong, but later, it feels like things couldn't have been truer and clearer than this.

Yet what does this all mean for a parent that is unaware?

Learning about your child's true identity and sexuality can come as a shock. You may end up blaming yourself or the company your child had. Even if you are a supporter of the LGBTQ+ community, you might react harshly to your child's coming out. You may reject your child and ask them to change, or you may show support and tell them that it's going to be alright.

Part of being understanding and supportive involves developing a true sense of how the world views them and treats them. You have already seen it but never experienced it firsthand. It may sound obvious to you, but you have to be willing to listen. The process of education begins with listening to the personal stories of people who have experienced stereotyping firsthand.

Make it your mission to learn more about the community, their history, struggle, terminologies, etc. that they still face complexes with today. For example, you can research the origins of a pride parade and related events. You are bound to come across historical events like the Stonewall riots in 1969; Harvey Milk and his contribution; the National March on Washington for Lesbian and Gay Rights in 1979; and many more. You will have a better idea of why people were protesting for equal rights over the years and how they came to celebrate diversity today. Knowing about the whole spectrum of gender identities can help you answer questions about your child, too.

However, be sure to not sound offensive or cumbersome toward your child if you fail to understand certain topics or mistake gender pronouns. The more you research, the better you will get.

Second, you must confront your prejudices. When you decide to be an understanding and supportive parent, you will need to change your bias and assumptions you held without knowledge against the LGBTQ+ community. Recall all the jokes you cracked about them, how you deliberately denied calling them by their desired pronouns, and how you looked down upon anyone with a same-sex partner. LGBTQ+ prejudices are often subtle and unnoticeable. You must accept that you were wrong and show your child that you are willing to work on your beliefs and overall bias.

Third, you need to check your privilege. We all enjoy some form of it without knowledge. It could be related to our skin color, education, social status, or physicality. Being privileged doesn't mean that you didn't have your share of struggles. It means that in some cases, you never have to think or worry about something while others have to worry about it all the time. For example, people of color worry about a lack of opportunities and rights in many fields. If you were born with a lighter skin tone, you rarely had to worry about being treated differently. Understanding your privilege will help you build compassion and empathy for those who don't have it. You will begin to see how oppressed and marginalized the LGBTQ+ community is.

Learn to speak up and put people in their right places when they utter something offensive. It could be your friends and family that say hurtful things. Speaking up may make the situation awkward, but it will also educate people. It will remind them that their insensitive remarks won't be welcomed or appreciated in your household. When you speak up, others will, too. Become an ally and build the courage to speak up so that you may educate others in the process.

Chapter 2:

Acceptance Comes Next

Depending on your family's cultural beliefs, you may question your child's gender identity and sexual orientation. Many parents are left wondering if it is something that they did that turned their child into a gay, lesbian, or transgender person If the child prefers same-sex partners, the parents become worried about carrying their generation forward and whether they will have grandkids or not. Some are worried about the treatment their child will receive in school, college, and the workplace. Many even feel ashamed to talk about it with their extended family and friends. Instead of being accepting and affectionate, they tell the child that it is definitely a phase they are going through and will soon be back on track. This is both humiliating and hurtful.

We must remember that the majority of the parents think of these questions out of love and concern for their child's emotional and mental well-being. However, the way they direct their responses and reactions may make the child think as if they are being rejected for who they are. Dr. Caitlyn Ryan, a clinical social worker and founder of the Family Acceptance Project at San Francisco State University, believes that it is natural for parents to mourn the loss of their expectations from their child. They may need some time to relax and breathe. After all, what they wanted for their child, from healthy relationships to a happy family, is shattered. They should never forget that healthy relationships, marriage, and children are still not off the table. The reality might look different, but it is still possible to achieve those goals (Ryan, 2008).

Therefore, you should practice acceptance. You must respect their decision to have a family of their own or not. Chances are that children who feel accepted and loved by their families are more likely to want something similar for themselves and their partners. If they are raised with love, acceptance, and affection, they will want to give the same love, care, and affection to someone tomorrow.

For now, take some time to learn what your child needs. You can show support for your LGBTQ+ child by accepting their reality with an open mind. Besides, their sexuality and gender identity don't make them any less likable. They are still the same they were a minute ago.

Family Acceptance Matters

As the world continues to accept the new gender norms and see the bigger picture, family realms should, too. With countries legalizing same-sex couples and marriages, as well as advocating for diversity in the workforce, families should be considerate of this new reality.

Dr. Ryan, during her research, conducted some studies on how a family's acknowledgment, consideration, and acceptance affect the well-being of LGBTQ+ children. She also looked at the effect of rejecting and hurtful behaviors on a child's well-being as well. One of her studies concluded that families who aren't supportive of their child's sexual and gender identity, despite believing that being gay or lesbianism is wrong, raise more admirable and confident children (Ryan, 2008). If families learn to support their children with diverse interests, it can have a significant, positive impact on their self-esteem and overall well-being.

On the other hand, families that aren't supportive and create toxicity in their child's lives raise children who are eight times at a higher risk for attempted suicide, six times more likely to suffer from chronic depression, and more than three times more likely to engage in drugs or unprotected sex (Ryan, 2008).

In another study in the same realm, she and her colleagues found out that family acceptance protects adolescents against suicidal behavior and substance abuse (Ryan et al., 2010). These children feel loved and taken care of, leading to higher self-esteem; healthy mental and emotional development; and social support.

How to Show Support

So how can you make it less difficult for them? How can you assure them of your love and acknowledgment? What can you do to show support and acceptance?

For starters, have a basic understanding of the broad spectrum of LGBTQ+ identities, respectfully. Once you are aware of their gender identity, start the conversation. Show interest in learning about who they are. A few places to have the conversation can be the dinner table while watching the news or when something related comes up. If your child feels hesitant in opening up, you can create stories about people of the same gender identity at your workplace and ease them into having the conversation by making the story relatable. For example, you can say something about how the person was so confused at first about the way they were feeling, how they battled those thoughts and gathered up the courage to come out, etc.

If you are still unsure about what they are going through, ask open-ended questions. Ask them to tell you how they feel or think. Let those responses guide your discussion. Ask them how you can be more supportive and what changes in behavior and treatment they expect from you. For instance, they may not want you to treat them as if they were ill or had a chronic disease. They don't want sympathetic eyes. Instead, they may want you to celebrate their uniqueness by treating them the same way you did earlier.

Second, talk positively about diversity and how it adds more color to life. Emphasize how being different means newness and change. Encourage dialogue about different cultures, races, and sexual orientations as well. Show them that, regardless of who they are, they continue to be beautiful and admirable.

Some days, you will find it impossible to gain trust, especially if your initial reaction was offensive and shocking. Now is the time to build trust. You can start small by getting to know their friends and things they are interested in. Being curious about their lives and wanting to be an active part of them speaks about your commitment and acceptance. This will also demonstrate how approachable you are. When your child thinks they can talk to you about anything, they will be more at ease with their sexual and gender orientation.

You can also be intrigued about their journey and experiences—as long as they feel comfortable speaking about them. For many children, learning about their sexual orientation and gender identity is an exciting moment. The confusion is finally clear. They feel like meeting themselves for the first time. Sharing that experience can indeed be a great way to exhibit acceptance.

Another way to accept them for who they are is by listening without argument or interruption. Many times, children feel unheard because the parent is busy with some housework or looking at their phones during conversations. Keep in mind that this is bigger than everything else. If your child has chosen to come out to you, they are seeking acceptance and approval. Don't reject them. Don't hurt their feelings by being involved half-heartedly. Listen when they open up about their struggles and concerns. Ensure your trust and support by being attentive and concerned. Assure them that your love for them won't change. Be more expressive of your affection toward them. They must, at all times, know that you love them unconditionally. Your child needs to know that their identity won't affect the relationship you have with them. Your acceptance and acknowledgment will ensure that.

In case you reacted poorly to their confession initially, apologize. There is nothing you can change about what happened, but you can decide what happens next. It starts with a genuine and straightforward apology. Open up about how you were shocked, confused, and somewhat angry about what happened, but you aren't anymore. You may have underestimated your child's capacity to fathom your initial reaction, but chances are, they already expected it. They might have rehearsed coming out to you a hundred times because of doing so. The point is that they will understand.

You can also find your child an LGBTQ+ role model among friends, celebrities, and extended family members to further show your support. Having a role model to look up to can give children the confidence to face the world and come out more confidently to their friends and family members. If they are young and look up to entertainers, celebrities like JoJo Siwa, Elliot Page, and Amandla Stenberg from *The Hunger Games* can serve as great motivators. They all had their fair share of hate and rejection from the world, but their strong-willed nature and refusal to bow down to others made them a star of another league. Eventually, people backed their stance and accepted them for who they are, proving that success and acceptance are achievable if one works for it passionately.

You must also check in with your child often to show support. Keeping an open line of communication is imperative. As an observer of their behavior, there will be several things that will be new to you. You can always ask them to keep you in the circle of how things are. It is common for children to explore their sexuality during their teen years. An open line of communication ensures that their actions and behaviors don't go unnoticed. Even if your child is changing or expressing themselves in new ways, staying in the loop allows you to be supportive. They might have more to share.

This brings us to the importance of encouraging self-expression in children. LGBTQ+ children often experiment with their choice of clothing or appearance. They might want to chop off their hair one day or dress like a boy with their father's shirt. Self-expression is the best way to help them experiment freely and openly. Let them come to terms with what suits them best on their own.

Whenever you notice any injustice, homophobic comments, or mistreatment toward your child, speak up. You need to become an active advocate for your child, especially at school. School is the one place children most often get bullied, and your child might too because they are different. Keep a vigilant eye on the treatment they are receiving at school and be open to discussing and bringing forward any case of harassment or bullying to the school administration. Your child, no matter how different, has every right to feel safe in the classroom. Also, stay in touch with their friends and teachers if you feel like your child may hide things from you. Speaking up for your child will put an end to bullying and unnecessary harassment before it gets worse.

Be welcoming of new people in your child's lives, especially love interests. Every child, at some point, has crushes and love interests. They connect with them on a deeper level, and as parents, we should be encouraging of that experience. Dating and romantic partners are often daunting for most parents, especially if they are with same-sex partners. However, parents shouldn't forget that it is an important part of their journey growing up, and they can't always rely on you alone. It is best to be involved and interested in their love lives but only with their permission. Some children don't like to share much, and if that is the case with your child, it is best to allow them their privacy. Allowing them some space involves opening your heart and house to them.

Chapter 3:

Fast-Forward to Tolerance

Tolerance and parenting don't go together well, especially when children are young and mischievous. They end up in all sorts of troubles—from putting their hands in sockets to forgetting to close the fridge after grabbing a treat. For parents with multiple kids, the struggle becomes even more challenging. Parents are on 24-hour duty, possibly angry, and tired to the bone.

When we talk about sexual orientation and gender identity, the reality isn't any different. In many homes, particularly ones that are on the religious spectrum, coming out to everyone as LGBTQ+ is courageous, to say the least. In conservative homes, there is no room for such bold self-expression, and many parents, therefore, outright reject their children. There have been cases where teenagers have felt trapped in their homes, wanting to run away because their parents aren't understanding. Many children want to leave town, fearing their mental peace and physical safety.

Patience and tolerance go a long way. Patience allows for better assimilation of the new reality in the house and helps parents make peace with it.

Above all, we are responsible for looking after our children and ensuring that they feel safe and looked after.

In this next chapter, we look at how patience can help parents form a stronger bond with their child that identifies themselves as a member of the LGBTQ+ community. We shall look at how being open to communication and becoming tolerant can provide our children a safe space to express themselves—regardless of what the world thinks of them.

Patience Is Your Ultimate Weapon

It can be hard to remain patient when your child comes up with the most absurd confession, but you have had an idea about it already, haven't you? You knew from the start that they were unlike others. From wanting to play with dolls to dressing up, you knew that your precious boy was different. However, you brushed off the thought, thinking you were overreacting. Now, that they come to you, claiming their true self, impatience is the last thing they need.

For parents, patience is truly a virtue. It takes guts to be accepting of something that you don't believe in. It's like telling someone that you saw aliens and expecting them to believe it. It can be hard to remain patient when your child is acting differently and doing things differently. If you come from a conservative, Jewish,

Christian, or Muslim household, there is little space for such expression. Since you have been brought up to believe that there is no such thing as being gay or lesbian and that these are just abnormalities in the brain, you are keen to change your child's gender identity and sexual orientation. In hopes of regaining their "natural mental state," you shove ideas toward them about how being LGBTQ+ is a sin. You bring them Bible verses that provide no valid proof that it is wrong to be who you are. You set them up on dates with their opposite gender, assuming the right boy/girl will set their mind straight.

Medical science has confirmed that being LGBTQ+ has nothing to do with any disability or abnormality in the mind. It isn't some unwanted release of chemicals that clouds the mind. Being gay isn't a conscious choice or preference. There are several biological factors involved, so why condemn them for something they have no say in?

Coming back to the topic of patience, parents must abstain from condemning, scrutinizing, and challenging their child's sexual orientation and gender identity. Instead, they should be tolerant of how they choose to express themselves. The minute we stop snapping at our children is the moment we start to listen to them. Challenging or questioning their identity only leads to saying things you are going to regret later. Patience is what takes more work. It means to not shatter or erupt—even when you feel like it.

As members of a family, you can both work out a way that promotes openness. Together, you can talk and set new expectations with your children. If the thought of your child being gay or a lesbian still upsets you, you can work out a strategy where they try their best to take things slow and allow you some time to come to terms with it. With patience, you can be more forgiving and accepting of your child's friends and romantic partners whenever they are around.

Only then can you create a deep and meaningful connection with your child where they feel loved and understood. Our patience shows that we trust our children to know the best and have confidence in their abilities. It reminds them that they are the makers of their future and have the leverage to decide what's best for them in their own time and space.

Providing a Judgment-Free Space

When a child opens up to a parent about how they feel different from the rest of their friends, it is a big step for them. It is filled with anxiety and fear about your reaction. It is also filled with hope that they will be accepted wholeheartedly. As a parent, your child needs to believe that their parents will be supportive of their decision and love them no matter what. They want validation for their anxieties rather than parents telling them that they are being delusional. Family acceptance and tolerance promote well-being. Listening to your child and approving their sense of self has great value.

Asking open-ended questions about how they feel and what the future looks like for them allows for better digestion for both the child and the parent. They can finally be on the same page with the new information and make the best of it. Open conversations about who they are, challenges they face, and what they expect from you can help children feel safe. They can express and share their emotions in a nonjudgmental space.

To provide them with one, below are some strategies that will help foster a welcoming and appreciative environment within your house where the child feels free to express their sexuality and identity in the way they intended to.

Point out unfair stereotypes seen in the media. Media has a powerful impact on our thinking. It builds perspective and modifies ideas. Our attitudes change based on what we see. Positive representation of the LGBTQ+ community can serve as a powerful tool in changing the mindset of people toward the community. However, equally important is to point out any discrimination against the LGBTQ+ community. If you notice an ad, film, or series discouraging and disregarding the feelings of LGBTQ+ people, don't hesitate in raising your voice against it. Use social media platforms to raise your voice and get others on board. Don't relax until you receive an apology from the regulatory body so that your child knows you fully support their self-expression. Be sure to bring up stories about social injustice at the workplace toward diverse people and discuss strategies to help them feel like a part of the family. Such discussions can lead to some meaningful insights for you as well as them.

If you have more than one child in the house, be sure to show respect toward everyone. Don't let your LGBTQ+ child feel like a stranger. Ensure that everyone in the house accepts and appreciates them for their diversity. Respect in the house is a confidence booster. When a child feels respected for who they are, their passions, and their goals, they can work on them with greater confidence and self-worth.

To do this, have a separate conversation with your other children and ask them to respect each other's differences. Don't allow anyone to harass or reject your LGBTQ+ child's beliefs. Enforce strong repercussions for anyone that tries to bring them down or shame them for being different.

In line with that, use appropriate pronouns for your child. If they choose to identify themselves differently, go with it. They shouldn't have to hide in the house. Make others aware of their decision so that other siblings don't make fun. Abstain from any homophobic or transphobic comments in the house.

Make your house LGBTQ+ friendly. This can mean inviting your child's friends over for lunch or snacks and having books and art by people that identify as LGBTQ+. You can easily browse authors and films online and bring them into your house.

You can also spend the weekend by participating in walks, fundraisers, and rallies—which support gay, lesbian, transgender, and queer people—as a family. This will send a clear message to the child of your support and appreciation. It will also strengthen the bond between you and cultivate a sense of positivity in the house.

Chapter 4:

Exposure to Age-Appropriate, Diverse Media

While talking about LGBTQ+ children, we often forget that others in the family need education as well. Siblings may experience trouble with the newness because their reality changes as well. Younger children have a difficult time coming to terms with their older brother or sister identifying themselves as gay, lesbian, asexual, pansexual, or bisexual.

Explaining to them the realities and struggles of an LGBTQ+ child may require some assistance, the best source being exposure to age-appropriate media. Awkward conversations can be held decently and respectfully where everyone feels a part of a team. With the right exposure at the proper time, we can prepare others in the house to wholeheartedly embrace their siblings in a positive manner.

In many households, gender identity and sexual preference talks are considered taboo. Young children are excused from these conversations, leaving them confused as to why their sibling is dressing or identifying themselves differently.

If you are a parent that wishes to raise children with a strong sense of morals, respect, and discipline, you can't avoid these uncomfortable but important conversations.

Exposure to diversity is a suitable practice. The research concludes that regular exposure or proximity to diverse cultures and people enhances learning and acceptance (Mann, 2014). It normalizes the idea of diversity in our minds, leading to a shift in our attitudes and beliefs. When we surround ourselves with more diverse people, we become more accepting of their existence and importance.

However, it can be difficult to explain to young children the different colors, shapes, and forms of diversity, so your best bet is exposure to the right media that depicts them in a constructive light.

Learning about diversity and homosexuality is important for children, as it teaches them to respect people from all ethical backgrounds, races, and cultures. They realize that not everyone is alike, and it is their differences that make them unique. Learning about diversity also makes them more empathetic. They stop judging or rejecting those who are different. This allows them to get along with everyone they meet, which is an important social trait to garner.

Finally, it also allows them to develop a sense of self. Teaching children about the different shades of the LGBTQ+ community also prevents bullying and harassment in schools and workplaces.

Why Teaching About Diversity Is Pivotal

According to one research report that examined North American children and the type of content they were exposed to daily through media outlets like Disney Channel, Disney Junior, Cartoon Network, PBS Kids, Nickelodeon, and Universal Kids, researchers made some shocking claims. After monitoring the content, they found out the following (Lemish & Johnson, 2019):

- Around 65% of the characters were white. On the contrary, female characters were more likely to be racially ambiguous. This goes on to show how the U.S. represents its makeup of population where 60% of the people are Caucasian, non-Hispanic, and non-Latinx.
- Despite the US being a woman-dominated country, only 38% of the lead characters were female.

- Male leads were more likely to solve problems using science, technology, or their physicality, whereas female leads were shown using magic.

- Objectification was another common theme in the majority of the shows where female characters were shown wearing revealing clothes to appear sexy. Those females are also thin, giving young girls the wrong inspiration to look up to. Given the number of cases of anorexia in the country and the obsession with size zero, this just goes on to prove how biased we are.

- Only 1% of the characters had a physical disability or chronic disease, despite it being a common occurrence in the U.S.

- Finally, there was little to no representation of gay, lesbian, or transgender characters as leads—not even in teen dramas. If we recall the dramas we watched while growing up, there was no concept of a gay or lesbian character, let alone them playing a lead role.

This suggests that from an early age, children are exposed to stereotyped ideals where men are portrayed as masculine and strong, whereas women are weak and feminine. Women are often left at the mercy of men in shining armor to come to their rescue. The lack of

LGBTQ+ representation leaves a wide gap between why we keep seeking acceptance for diverse communities and why we fail to accept them.

Lack of exposure to the LGBTQ+ community, their demands, and struggles also leave children questioning their sexual orientation and confused. If they were provided strong role models to look up to, their struggles would be fewer and less complex.

Lack of LGBTQ+ representation in the media leads to psychological outcomes for those who identify as LGBTQ+. Not only do they feel negatively portrayed, but they feel like their sense of self is deliberately left out.

Therefore, as a society, we need to push educational institutions, media channels, and those in power to discuss and bring issues of bias, diversity, and discrimination to light. With appropriate representation, we can urge middle schools and high schools to implement laws against discrimination and create a safe space for children belonging to all minority groups.

With mainstream representation, it will be easier for parents to initiate conversations about diversity in their homes, leading to a rise in a sensible and empathic population. In a world that seeks collaboration, this social skill can pay off well.

Yet a lack of representation isn't the only reason. As a parent, we think that our children are too young for these complex topics, so we delay exposing them to such notions. This only leads to more injustices because important issues keep getting brushed under the rug. Children, from an early age, have a keen sense of fairness. They are drawn to right over wrong, honesty over falsehood, and comfort over discomfort.

Racial differences aren't hidden from them either. From the naive age of three, they begin to notice physical characteristics between a boy and a girl such as long hair, sandals over sneakers, and dresses over a shirt. They become curious about skin color and hair texture around the same age. By the time they enter kindergarten, they can differentiate between different ethnic and racial groups.

Find Teachable Moments

The good news is that this lack of representation can be reversed if we allow our children to view age-appropriate media that depicts LGBTQ+ characters in all their glory. We can harness their desires for fairness and equality for all by giving them a chance to witness and feel what it is like to be on the other end of things. We can initiate conversations about discrimination, socio-economic status, and LGBTQ+ communities through films, books, and shows. If your family watches television a lot, don't be a parent that shuns their child away from anything remotely homosexual. Whether you allow it or not, there is a chance that they are exposed to it already at school or online. However, you can choose how they view and treat them. You can either raise bullies or advocates that raise their voice when they see any injustice happen. Surely, you would want to raise the latter kind. So how can you do that? Let's find out.

First, you must point out the lack of opportunities LGBTQ+ celebrities and athletes receive because of their gender identity and sexual orientation. The best way to do so is to go on a drive with your child in your neighborhood and look at advertisements placed all around town. Look at whose face is placed on a billboard and why. You are most likely to find zero ads featuring an LGBTQ+ individual. That alone should get the conversation going about how unjust the system is.

Turn to shows and movies for discussion about the challenges and struggles people of the LGBTQ+ community face. The following are some classic examples and age-appropriate movies to enjoy as a family with your preteens and teenagers:

- *Out*
- *The Most Dangerous Year*
- *In A Heartbeat*
- *Rosaline*
- *Tyler*
- *Love, Simon*

Also, have an abundance of books written by LGBTQ+ authors around the house. Show your children that LGBTQ+ individuals are equally qualified, creative, and intelligent in their area of interest. For younger children, you can start them on books and shows like, *The Adventures of Honey & Leon*, *Pride: The Story of Harvey Milk and the Rainbow Flag*, *Zenobia July*, etc. All these books feature LGBTQ+ protagonists dealing with their own set of unique problems and upsets.

You can take part in various pride parades, DIY badges, art, and create T-shirts for the event to offer support. You can even take home-baked delicacies for the event organizers to show your appreciation for them. Not only will the preparation get the kids excited, but their exposure to the LGBTQ+ community will also increase. This will lead to acceptance in the long run where your children will no longer see them as different.

Chapter 5:

Becoming an Advocate

As primary caregivers and parents, we need to stick up for our children. On one hand, we need to provide them the tools and confidence to deal with their problems themselves, and on another we need to be prepared to speak up for them in case their voices go unheard. Only then can they grow into the amazing adult they are destined to be. When it comes to supporting your child among their circle of friends or school, parents feel reluctant, to say the least. They get lost in the sea of what-if scenarios, leaving children unsupported and alone.

When we talk about an LGBTQ+ child, the stakes are even higher. It can be confusing. What kind of support does my child need? How can I bring up issues related to their sexuality and gender identity without being too outspoken? How can I ensure that my child feels safe in their surroundings?

This is where becoming an advocate comes in. An advocate is someone that speaks on behalf of others to gather more noise and set things straight. Every parent is automatically an advocate for their child. They can't see them getting hurt, harassed, or bullied, but what are the limitations of being an advocate for an LGBTQ+ child?

Navigating the deep waters of advocacy can sometimes leave parents feeling overwhelmed. They can feel stuck in a typhoon, hopeless, and at the mercy of school administration and educators. Some educators aren't as open and accepting of diverse gender identities and thus, they might not be the most ideal person to reach out to concerning your child's safety and mental well-being.

Despite being a challenge, parents must become an advocate for their children. They must put trust in their abilities to raise their voice on behalf of their children. Advocating for an LGBTQ+ child takes a whole new level of courage. It is something that isn't widely accepted and acknowledged. Although many schools are putting into practice laws and regulations for the safety of LGBTQ+ children, how those laws are enforced matters.

In smaller towns and counties, children may continue to suffer because of a lack of adherence to those laws, given that there aren't any in place. In that case, even for a parent, the struggle can be real.

Why Advocacy?

As your child's only advocate, a lot falls on your shoulders. If you happen to be soft-spoken by nature, chances are that you hate confrontation. You may have trouble putting forth your case and why it means the world to you. Needless to say, it will be difficult for you to advocate for your child when you feel like you are against the world. But, with some sound preparation and confidence, you can walk in armed with reasons why your child should be treated equally. You can even bring up concerns and make suggestions.

The reasons to become an advocate for your child are many. First, someone needs to take charge and responsibility if your child is treated badly at school. You need to inform the authorities about the type of mistreatment and how it is affecting your child's self-esteem and confidence. Second, many school districts haven't felt the need to place stringent and clear anti-harassment and anti-bullying laws in place because no one has come forth suggesting them. Most of the time, children don't report harassment out of fear and more bullying. They prefer to stay quiet and mind their business, despite being continuously humiliated. By raising your voice against it, schools can hold seminars and workshops to help children treat everyone equally.

They can also take on counselors that specialize in dealing with such discrimination in schools and help kids who are facing these cope with them. They can have a thorough chat with the bullies and hold them accountable for their actions.

Raising your voice for your child's rights will also help other parents and children come forward. You can become a trailblazer and demand more attention and care for children who identify as different. Other parents will also become more aware and respectable toward LGBTQ+ children and their parents. Many households deter children from befriending peers who are different, believing such children are a bad influence.

Becoming an advocate for your child will also let the educators know your child better and ensure equal treatment in and out of the classroom. When you are not present, they can serve as your child's guardians and encourage self-expression without fear.

Becoming a Powerful Instrument of Change

Becoming an instrument for change is how you become an effective advocate for your LGBTQ+ child. As stated earlier, you don't need a set of skills and expertise to advocate for your child's rights. What you need are the things mentioned below.

You must know what your child desires. Have they come out to their friends yet? Are they planning to do so at any point? Are they confident about disclosing their identity? What purpose would you becoming an advocate serve them? What is the outcome they expect your advocacy to deliver?

These are some of the questions that you must ponder over before reaching out to the authorities and educators. If the child isn't comfortable about sharing their identity with the world yet, let them take things at their pace. If they are being harassed or bullied, sit down and devise strategies that would help them counter their bullies and put an end to the harassment.

What laws govern their protection and safety? Research state laws that guarantee their protection and safety. At the same time, also research what punishments and fines are put in place for people who verbally or physically harass LGBTQ+ people. Title IX of the Education Amendments of 1972 bans discrimination on the basis of sex by public schools. This includes boys who wish to wear makeup and girls who like to dress like boys. According to the law, the school administration or anyone else can't "out" them for being different. Using the law as your primary weapon will help you communicate your child's rights in a more effective manner. If the school administration fails to take notice or stop the bullying and harassment, you can take them to court for discouraging self-expression in kids (Office for Civil Rights [OCR], 2021).

Raise your voice and make it loud and clear. Use the right platforms to let others hear you, too. You need to find support to strengthen your case. The more noise you gather, the more effective your stance is. Invite other children who identify as different into your house and ask them to share their stories, concerns, and struggles. Use your social media to advocate for them and talk about the mental and emotional challenges that come with it.

Follow through with your progress and the impact it is creating. If it seems ineffectual, come up with a different strategy. You need to keep going as long as everyone at school is aware of your stance. Engage your child's teachers by sending them a text, email, or note asking for an ideal time for a talk. Talk them through about what your child is experiencing at school and what you plan to do about it. Allowing them to be a part of this conversation will help them raise the issue with higher authorities. If speaking to a teacher seems futile, you can get other parents in a similar situation to join. Having someone to talk to about the challenges you face can relieve you of some worry.

If you find people mispronouncing someone's gender, be quick to point it out. Even when you are talking about someone that isn't in the room, they deserve respect. Avoid using racially charged language and stop others from doing so, too.

You can do much more by becoming an instrument of change in your workplace. For example, you can welcome diversity in your house, neighborhood, and workplace. If you are in charge of employees, an act as simple as updating everyone's email signatures to include pronouns will start the much-needed conversation.

To advocate for your child in public spaces, you can proudly wear a pride badge or pin on your shirt. This will let everyone know that you aren't ashamed of allowing your child to be who they are. You can use social media, as stated before, to educate others and unite marginalized groups that lack support systems. This means showing support for children with learning or physical disabilities, children that suffer from racism and discrimination, etc. The more people you gather, no matter what their struggles, the greater your voice will be.

Chapter 6:

Attending to Feelings of Loneliness and Bullying

In a 2017 article by the *Washington Post*, author and former Surgeon General, Vivek H. Murthy, called emotional well-being and loneliness as one of the biggest pandemics people face (McGregor, 2017). You will be surprised to know that a significant majority of the population in the U.S. and U.K. call TV their only means of interaction with the outer world. An average American faces isolation and disconnectedness several times in their lives. Some of the common culprits include age discrimination, busy work schedules, geographic remoteness, and broken family dynamics. Yet there is a bigger chunk of youngsters, adults, and seniors that experience this remoteness and social isolation almost every day of their lives. The LGBTQ+ community is at a higher risk of loneliness, bullying, harassment, and isolation in schools and offices because of their true representation.

They are made to think that they deserve to be alone and harassed because of the way they choose to live. Although there hasn't been much research into exploring the core of the disruption in an LGBTQ+ child's mental and emotional well-being, it isn't hard to guess, given the treatment they receive for being different. Schools and workplaces haven't been as accommodating as they claim to be, leaving young children without friends and people to bond with.

Social isolation, followed by bullying and harassment, makes children feel unwanted and unaccepted by their peers and family members. This social isolation is sometimes direct and active or indirect and passionate. This is why social exclusion is an important topic to discuss:

> Social exclusion is a complex and [multidimensional] process. It involves the lack or denial of resources, rights, goods and services, and the inability to participate in the normal relationships and activities, available to the majority of people in a society, whether in economic, social, cultural[,] or political arenas. (Levitas et al., 2007)

LGBTQ+ children are often the last people picked in group projects because no one wants to be associated with them. Such injustice damages their self-esteem. These children never receive the chance to prove their skills and expertise, further injuring their confidence.

It is less direct and passive when LGBTQ+ children feel that they aren't respected enough and that nobody wants to hang out with them. They feel unseen and unheard because people don't see them as equals. Their gender identity is often picked as a subject of ridicule.

LGBTQ+ teenagers unable to express their sexuality openly like their peers suffer social isolation that comprises four dimensions. There is lack of support from their peers, limited contact with the LGBTQ+ community, victimization, and social withdrawal. There comes a point when they deliberately begin to avoid social events, fearing being called out for their different sexual preference and identity.

According on one study that reviewed four articles, sexual minorities report higher ratings of loneliness than those who come labeled as heterosexuals (Gorczynski & Fasoli, 2021).

Many children are victims of shaming and bullying because of their sexual preference. This can be disheartening for them. As a reaction to coming out as LGBTQ+, they may face social isolation from their peers or humiliation and bullying from others. This is the time to tend to their feelings and remind them that they aren't wrong for being themselves. Reassure their decision, accept them wholeheartedly, and let them know that they aren't alone in this fight.

Your Child Isn't Alone

Older LGBTQ+ individuals are more prone to being lonely, single, isolated, and withdrawn from contact with relatives. The older population is also less likely to engage with local services, as they feel discriminated against by professionals for the way they choose to live.

Certainly, this isn't the type of life you imagine your child to have. Apart from social isolation, bullying, and harassment, they also suffer legal inequality, daily abuse, and social withdrawal from their loved ones.

If you don't believe this, put on the TV, read a billboard, or watch a film—you will find messages celebrating heterosexuality. Very few will be found under the LGBTQ+ acronym. Collectively, they trust upon the idea that diverse people aren't viewed as equals. This lack of representation can be disheartening for most children and teenagers, especially the ones residing in rural areas with limited options to explore their sexuality. There is an increased likelihood of social injustice, rejection, and loneliness if you are an LGBTQ+ youth in a small town or county. It isn't just the geographical isolation that they face; people also happen to be narrow-minded. According to one survey, gay farmers have had a difficult time in finding partners and acceptance from their loved ones (Pritchard, 2018).

What your child needs is your support through and through. They need you to stand up for them and raise your voice.

If you notice them being bullied, pushed over, and assaulted verbally, don't let that go unnoticed. The only way you can put an end to their misery is by taking a stand for them. Involving the school administration and their primary educators is the first step. Read up on the rules and laws against bullying and discrimination and prepare a case to present in front of the school district. If you happen to be in an area that offers limited support, file a petition, and get people from your community, friends, and neighborhood to join.

Take the petition to the streets if your message is ignored. This will create awareness and give more people, in a similar situation, a chance to be a part of an important movement.

You can also reach out to LGBTQ+ support groups like:

- GLMA: Health Professionals Advancing LGBTQ Equality
- Parents, Families, Friends, and Allies of Lesbians and Gays (PFLAG)
- Gay, Lesbian & Straight Education Network (GLSEN)
- Gay and Lesbian Alliance Against Defamation (GLAAD)
- Advocates for Youth (AFY): LGBTQ Resources for Professionals

These groups and programs help LGBTQ+ children and parents find the support they need to start a ripple effect of change. Reading about the personal struggles of others and finding out ways to support your child's self-expression is what these support groups offer. You can even reach out to professionals and prepare your case against your child's school administration if your child continues to get bullied and socially isolated for being different.

How to Offer Help

As a parent, it is natural for you to want to protect your child, but you can't be with them all the time. How can you be with them—even when you aren't present physically? In this final section, we look at how parents can offer emotional support and help to their LGBTQ+ children.

Become a Confidant

For any child exploring their sexuality and gender identity, what they need the most is someone they can confide in without feeling judged. Allow yourself to take on that role and provide your children a safe space to express themselves with you. Be available and listen actively to what they feel and experience. Work out ways that they can feel less isolated. If you feel you aren't the right person to offer emotional support, find someone that has gone through something similar. Encourage your child to make friends with people who have diverse preferences as themselves and form an alliance. That friend, partner, or mentor should be someone that they can reach out to in times of need. If there is no one they can relate to at their school or place of work, encourage them to join LGBTQ+ groups and forums to seek friends from all over the globe. Sometimes, having someone to talk to and vent out your feelings to is the best cure.

Make Your Home a Safe Haven

Children experiencing confusion and social isolation can feel relieved and at peace when they are surrounded by people who appreciate and encourage self-expression. Make your home a friendly space for LGBTQ+ where your child can explore themselves. Invite people who are different to promote diversity and reassure your child that they shouldn't have to hide themselves when around you or their siblings. Make a note to remind everyone to respect one another—regardless of their sexuality. This will create a positive and harmonious environment in your home where your child feels included, validated, and appreciated.

Validate Feelings

It's also important that your child knows you appreciate their self-expression and choices. Your role should be of a supporter and ally. LGBTQ+ children often report feeling judged by their family members on many occasions. Some parents feel ashamed to take them to social events or tell them to hide their sexuality—don't be like that. End all the blaming and guilt that you might have put them through in the past for being themselves. Validate their feelings and tell them that you understand what they are going through. Tell stories about friends and colleagues you worked with who were different. Keep the channels of communication open and frequently ask them how you can be of help.

Help Them Socialize

Research support groups and alliances in your area that acknowledge homosexuality openly and appreciatively. Take your child to social events that celebrate homosexuality. This includes pride walks, marathons, and charity events hosted by LGBTQ+ groups year-round. If they continue to experience bullying and social isolation at school, finding another space to be themselves and feel at peace will be rewarding. Engaging in social activities that foster and celebrate diversity can be a great way to blow off some steam. It will help children find like-minded people and expand their circle of friends who "get" it.

Finally, don't forget to remind them that things will get better—even if they seem terrible now. We have come a long way from shunning gays and lesbians to accepting them openly. There is still a long way to go, but the future seems much more hopeful for them. As more and more companies, schools, and industries open their hearts and spaces for diverse people, there will soon come a time where they will be treated like any other heterosexual being and celebrated for being themselves.

Chapter 7:

What Am I Doing Wrong?

There are some things that parents raising an LGBTQ child forget. For example, they forget that their child's gender expression isn't an act of defiance or rebellion. They aren't trying to bring shame to your family. They forget how it isn't the child's fault that they feel different in their body or are attracted to people the society doesn't deem right for them.

In this final chapter, we shall debunk some common myths to understand and respect the LGBTQ+ community as a whole. This piece of advice is for everyone—not just for parents raising LGBTQ+ children.

Myth: My child is homosexual because they were sexually abused or lacked strong sex role models growing up.

Fact: No evidence suggests that this is true. Your child's sexual orientation has nothing to do with a lack of a strong parental role model or abuse. According to The American Psychiatric Association's fact sheet, sexual abuse doesn't appear to be anymore prevalent among LGBTQ+ children than in children that identify as heterosexuals (Bradford et al., 2000).

Myth: Being gay is a choice, and no one is born gay.

Fact: Both of these statements are false. Modern science has yet to find evidence that being gay is a personal choice. However, multiple studies suggest that homosexuality is a mix of biological and environmental forces. In one of the largest studies of its time, Swedish researchers studied twins and their behaviors. One of them was gay while the other was heterosexual. Researchers concluded that homosexual behavior was largely shaped by environmental factors and genetics (Långström et al., 2010).

Myth: Being gay is a mental disorder.

All professional mental health organizations have been on record saying that homosexuality has nothing to do with a mental abnormality in the brain. According to The American Psychological Association (2003), being gay is as healthy as being straight. In 1975, the organization issued a statement claiming that homosexuals are equally good with judgment, reliability, and have social and vocational capabilities.

Myth: We can cure homosexuality.

Fact: There has been some talk about referral and reparative surgeries proving to be effective in "curing" homosexuality. However, they all have been untrue and ineffective. Years of research into the subject have proven that it is highly unlikely one can change their gender identity and sexual preference. Many leading mental health and counseling organizations are against the involvement and usage of any such conversion therapies.

Myth: I did something wrong.

Fact: As a parent, let this be said once and for all: Nothing you did made your child an LGBTQ+ child. Self-blame and guilt are common and natural responses. Parents must know that a child's sexual orientation isn't learned behavior. Just as you couldn't have caused your child to be straight, you can't cause your child to become gay, bisexual, or pansexual.

Myth: There is no harm in referring to your trans child by their birth name.

Fact: You indeed want your child to be the same. Your love for them hasn't changed, so why change who they are? This is what the LGBTQ+ supporters call deadnaming. Referring to your trans child by their previous name after they have chosen a new one can trigger anxiety. For years, they have tried to escape their bodies. Calling them by their dead name is, therefore, both disrespectful and unwanted.

With these myths and facts in mind, below are some more tips to stop the blunders we make in our minds about our LGBTQ+ children.

For example, we try to prevent them from expressing their gender in public or family events because we think the knowledge will make others uncomfortable. Doing so only makes your child feel like they aren't part of the group or that they are doing something wrong by being themselves.

We prevent them from making gender-diverse friends and block access to gender-diverse activities and resources. Lack of like-minded people in their social circle can lead to social isolation and loneliness. Having to share their experiences with someone that has experienced the same is a great way to connect and form stronger bonds.

At times, we allow others in the family, like other siblings and cousins, to belittle and ridicule our LGBTQ+ child in the name of fun. It might seem lighthearted entertainment for others, but it isn't for your child. Don't allow anyone in your family or friend group to isolate, harass, or ridicule your child. Watch out for bullies and harassers masked as friends and guardians.

Conclusion

It is difficult to define what it means to be a parent. The role is so multilayered that it is hard to put into words. Every culture, generation, and race puts different parameters to it. Many of you reading this would be biological parents. Some of you may have taken the role after the biological parent disappeared. You could be a grandparent, aunt, or uncle reading this. A few of you might be a foster parent, group home provider, or adoptive parent.

No matter where you fit in the many roles of parental care, one thing is certain: You are doing your best and putting your everything into it. No one can deny that. You are an exceptionally accommodating and sensible parent that knows what's best for their child.

Parental figures help children shape their identities and attitudes. They support them in developing their values, responsibility, and sense of self. Being a parent means you provide for your child—not just food and shelter but also safety and protection. It's protection from anyone and everyone that tries to bring them down or make them question themselves.

This includes being there for them when you don't agree with them as well. For many parents, their child's "coming out" confession isn't appreciated initially.

They experience a wave of shock in their systems, leaving them unprepared for what's to come. Things and expectations indeed change. Your once-beloved boy wants to be called a girl from now on, or they want to be in relationships with same-sex partners. This creates confusion and some resistance. Households that don't promote or appreciate homosexuality openly are the hardest to change.

This is one area that this book tries to help parents with: adjusting to the new changes and supporting their LGBTQ+ child—from speaking about the initial shock reaction to coming to terms with it; from connecting with your children to supporting them; and from appreciating their decision to advocating for them in schools, public places, and with extended family.

It talks about how we can prevent bullying and harassment by using the right platforms to raise our voices in their support. Exposure to appropriate media that builds on positive messages is another theme we explored along with coping with social isolation and loneliness that children experience after coming out.

Let this book serve as an important guide to navigate your new reality and ensure that your children feel loved, supported, and appreciated for owning their true selves.

Thank you for giving this book a read. I hope you loved reading it as much as I enjoyed writing it. It would make me the happiest person on earth if you would take a moment to leave an honest review. All you have to do is visit the site where you purchased this book: It's that simple! The review doesn't have to be a full-fledged paragraph; a few words will do. Your few words will help others decide if this is what they should be reading as well. Thank you in advance, and best of luck with your parenting adventures. Every moment is a joyous one with a child.

References

American Psychological Association [APA]. (2003, May 28). *Being Gay Is Just as Healthy as Being Straight.* American Psychological Association. https://www.apa.org/research/action/gay

Being an advocate for your child. (n.d.). FamilyConnect. https://familyconnect.org/education/know-your-rights/being-an-advocate-for-your-child/

Being an advocate for your child. (2021, September 8). Raising Children Network. https://raisingchildren.net.au/school-age/school-learning/working-with-schools-teachers/being-an-advocate

Bering, J. (2012). Is your child gay? *Scientific American Mind, 23*(3), 50–53. https://doi.org/10.1038/scientificamericanmind0712-50

Boyington, A. (2020, February 16). *Become your child's advocate: 10 actionable tips for parents.* Amy Boyington. https://amyboyington.com/childs-advocate

Bradford, J. B., Cahill, S., Grasso, C., & Makadon, H. J. (2000). *How to gather data on sexual orientation and gender identity in clinical settings.* The Fenway Institute. https://lgbtqiahealtheducation.org/wp-content/uploads/policy_brief_how_to_gather.pdf

Carroll, N. (2020, December 5). *7 ways you can be a better LGBTQ+ ally.* Students. https://www.ucl.ac.uk/students/news/2020/dec/7-ways-you-can-be-better-lgbtq-ally

Chodon, T. (2021, September 11). *How parents can be more accepting of their child's sexual orientation - times of india.* The Times of India. https://timesofindia.indiatimes.com/life-style/parenting/moments/how-parents-can-be-more-accepting-of-their-childs-sexual-orientation/articleshow/86093379.cms

Coming out: Information for parents of LGBT teens. (2019). HealthyChildren.org. https://www.healthychildren.org/English/ages-stages/teen/dating-sex/Pages/Four-Stages-of-Coming-Out.aspx

Drummond, K. D., Bradley, S. J., Peterson-Badali, M., & Zucker, K. J. (2008). A follow-up study of girls with gender identity disorder. *Developmental Psychology*, *44*(1), 34–45. https://doi.org/10.1037/0012-1649.44.1.34

GLAAD. (2011, September 5). *Is your child gay?* GLAAD. https://www.glaad.org/resources/ally/3

Gorczynski, P., & Fasoli, F. (2021). Loneliness in sexual minority and heterosexual individuals: A comparative meta-analysis. *Journal of Gay & Lesbian Mental Health*, 1–18. https://doi.org/10.1080/19359705.2021.1957742

Griffin, C. (2012, June 7). *HRC releases landmark survey of LGBT youth*. Human Rights Campaign. https://www.hrc.org/press-releases/hrc-releases-landmark-survey-of-lgbt-youth

Habacon, A. E. (n.d.). 13 tips on how to talk to children about diversity and difference. *Inclusive Excellence Strategy Solutions Inc.* https://www.aldenhabacon.com/13-tips-how-to-talk-to-children-about-diversity

Hanlon, P. (2018, September 14). *Isolation and LGBTQ youth: Social, psychological and financial implications | new england psychologist*. New England Psychologist. https://www.nepsy.com/articles/leading-stories/isolation-and-lgbtq-youth-social-psychological-and-financial-implications/

Hansen, I., & Madden, H. (2022, January 14). *How to accept that your child is gay, lesbian or bisexual*. WikiHow. https://www.wikihow.com/Accept-That-Your-Child-is-Gay,-Lesbian-or-Bisexual

Harris, J. (2019, July 2). How isolation leads to loneliness. *LGBT Foundation.* https://lgbt.foundation/news/how-isolation-leads-to-loneliness/317

Healthwise Staff. (2020, September 23). *Your teen's sexual orientation and gender identity.* Www.uofmhealth.org. https://www.uofmhealth.org/health-library/te7288

Iniguez, A., & Batavia, A. (2021, June 8). *10 myths about the LGBTQ+ community debunked.* Www.thoughtworks.com. https://www.thoughtworks.com/insights/blog/10-myths-about-lgbtq-community-debunked

Kansas State University. (2005, December 5). Early exposure to diversity good for children. *Www.newswise.com.* https://www.newswise.com/articles/early-exposure-to-diversity-good-for-children

King, S. (2020, June 25). *Talking to kids about gender and sexual orientation.* Www.chop.edu.

https://www.chop.edu/news/health-tip/talking-to-kids-about-gender-and-sexual-orientation

Långström, N., Rahman, Q., Carlström, E., & Lichtenstein, P. (2010). Genetic and environmental effects on same-sex sexual behavior: A population study of twins in sweden. *Archives of Sexual Behavior*, *39*(1), 75–80. https://doi.org/10.1007/s10508-008-9386-1

Lemish, D., & Johnson, C. R. (2019). *The landscape of children's television in the US & canada* (pp. 1–20). International Central Institute for Youth and Educational Television. https://static1.squarespace.com/static/5c0da585da02bc56793a0b31/t/5cb8ce1b15fcc0e19f3e16b9/1555615269351/The+Landscape+of+Children%27s+TV.pdf

Levinson, J. (2020, March 5). *Why diversity in children's media is so important*. Psychology in Action. https://www.psychologyinaction.org/psycholo

gy-in-action-1/2020/3/5/why-diversity-in-childrens-media-is-so-important

Levitas, R., Pantazis, C., Fahmy, E., Gordon, D., Lloyd-Reichling, E., & Patsios, D. (2007). The multi-dimensional analysis of social exclusion.

Mann, L. (2014, December 2). *Cultural diversity pays off, for kids of all ages.* Chicagotribune.com. https://www.chicagotribune.com/lifestyles/sc-fam-1209-children-diverse-neighborhood-20141202-story.html

McGregor, J. (2017, October 4). *This former surgeon general says there's a 'loneliness epidemic' and work is partly to blame.* The Washington Post. https://www.washingtonpost.com/news/on-leadership/wp/2017/10/04/this-former-surgeon-general-says-theres-a-loneliness-epidemic-and-work-is-partly-to-blame/

Myths that stigmatize LGBTQ people. (n.d.). Strong Family Alliance. Retrieved February 8, 2022, from https://www.strongfamilyalliance.org/parent-guide/essential-info/myths-that-stigmatize-lbgtq-people/#myth10

Office for Civil Rights [OCR]. (2021, October 27). *Title IX of the Education Amendments of 1972*. U.S. Department of Health & Human Services. https://www.hhs.gov/civil-rights/for-individuals/sex-discrimination/title-ix-education-amendments/index.html

Pallarés-Santiago, F. (2019, June 27). *6 ways to become a better LGBTQ ally*. Oprah Daily. https://www.oprahdaily.com/life/relationships-love/a28159555/how-to-be-lgbtq-ally/

Pritchard, E.-L. (2018, April 30). *Countryfile praised for uncovering heartbreaking struggles of gay farmers*. Country Living. https://www.countryliving.com/uk/wellbeing/a19871317/countryfile-struggles-gay-farmer/

Rasmussen, T. (2019, January 17). *How to tackle loneliness if you're LGBTQIA+*. Www.refinery29.com. https://www.refinery29.com/en-gb/2018/02/190556/lgbt-loneliness-support

Ryan, C. (2008). *Supportive families, healthy children: Helping families with lesbian, gay, bisexual and transgender children* (pp. 1–24). San Francisco State University.

Ryan, C., Russell, S. T., Huebner, D., Diaz, R., & Sanchez, J. (2010). Family acceptance in adolescence and the health of LGBT young adults. *Journal of Child and Adolescent Psychiatric Nursing, 23*(4), 205–213. https://doi.org/10.1111/j.1744-6171.2010.00246.x

Schlatter, E., & Steinback, R. (2011, February 11). 10 anti-gay myths debunked. *Intelligent Report.* https://www.splcenter.org/fighting-hate/intelligence-report/2011/10-anti-gay-myths-debunked

Sexual attraction and orientation (for teens) - kidshealth. (2012). Kidshealth.org. https://kidshealth.org/en/teens/sexual-orientation.html

Smelser, N. J. (2001). *International encyclopedia of the social & behavioral sciences / 10 [H]*. Elsevier, Pergamon.

Spiegelhalter, D. (2015, April 5). *Is 10% of the population really gay?* The Guardian.

Spiegler, J. (2016, June 16). *Teaching young children about bias, diversity, and social justice.* Edutopia. https://www.edutopia.org/blog/teaching-young-children-social-justice-jinnie-spiegler

Stewart, K. (2011, April 25). *Why are so many gay teens depressed?* EverydayHealth.com. https://www.everydayhealth.com/depression/why-are-so-many-gay-teens-depressed.aspx

Tips for parents of LGBTQ youth. (2019). Johns Hopkins Medicine. https://www.hopkinsmedicine.org/health/wellness-and-prevention/tips-for-parents-of-lgbtq-youth

Understand your child better with these child psychology tips. (n.d.). Child Development Institute. Retrieved February 2, 2022, from https://childdevelopmentinfo.com/child-psychology/#gs.nvgxsj

Why accepting your LGBTQ child matters—and how to start. (2009). OptionB.org. https://optionb.org/articles/why-accepting-your-lgbtq-child-matters-and-how-to-start

Youth Engaged 4 Change. (2015). *Being an ally to LGBT people.* Youth.gov. https://engage.youth.gov/resources/being-ally-lgbt-people

www.ingramcontent.com/pod-product-compliance
Lightning Source LLC
LaVergne TN
LVHW051017080826
845145LV00009B/2673

* 9 7 8 1 9 5 6 0 1 8 3 2 5 *